THE ADVENTURES OF
ROBINSON CRUSOE

By Daniel Defoe

**Retold by
ANGELA WILKES**

**Illustrated by
PETER DENNIS**

Series editor: Heather Amery

Long ago in England there lived a boy called Robinson Crusoe. He wanted to be a sailor, but his father would not let him go to sea.

"You must stay at home and work hard," he said. Robinson decided that when he was older he would run away from home.

One day, a few years later, he was walking round a port when he met a friend who was going to sea. "Why don't you come?" said the friend.

Crusoe agreed to go at once. He was so excited, he forgot to send a message to his father. He boarded the ship and soon it set sail.

Crusoe never returned home. He sailed all round the world. Then he decided to live in Brazil, bought some land and planted tobacco.

He worked hard for many years. He sold the tobacco he grew and became a very rich man. But he still wanted to travel.

One day some friends asked him to go with them on a voyage to Africa to trade for gold and ivory. Crusoe was eager to go to sea again.

When their ship was ready Crusoe and his friends set sail. For twelve days the sea was calm, but then the wind began to blow hard.

Huge waves crashed over the ship's decks, snapping the masts and tearing the sails. The ship was caught in a hurricane. After a few days

it hit a sandbank. Fearing it might sink, the men decided to abandon ship. They lowered a boat and began to row away.

3

The wind blew harder and huge waves broke over the boat, filling it with water. The men pulled hard at the oars, hoping to reach land.

Suddenly the boat tilted and slid down the side of a gigantic wave. The boat turned over, throwing all the men into the water.

Crusoe felt himself sinking. He held his breath and swam to the surface. Then a wave lifted him and he saw land. He swam hard.

He had not gone far when the waves threw him against a rock. Crusoe clung to it. He waited for a break in the waves, then swam on.

At last he reached the bottom of a cliff. Panting, he climbed upwards. The waves crashed below him. Crusoe did not look down.

At the top of the cliff he sat down. "What will become of me?" he thought. All he had in his pockets was a knife, a pipe and tobacco.

Crusoe was very thirsty. He searched for fresh water and found a stream. It was getting dark, so he looked for a safe place to sleep.

He decided that in a tree he would be out of reach of wild animals. He chose one with spreading branches, climbed up and fell asleep.

Next morning Crusoe looked out from his tree. The tide had washed the ship nearer to the shore. "I shall go out to it," thought Crusoe.

He climbed down from the tree and went to the beach. There he found some shoes and a hat. They were the only signs of his friends.

"I'm alone, but lucky to be alive," Crusoe thought sadly. "But how long shall I survive here?" He decided to swim out to the ship.

The ship was not far off. But when Crusoe reached it he found it lay high out of the water and he did not know how to climb aboard.

He swam round the ship and saw a rope hanging down. After a struggle Crusoe caught hold of it and pulled himself up on to the ship.

He went straight to the store room. All the food was still dry. Crusoe opened a box of biscuits. He was very hungry.

Next he decided to make a raft to carry things back to the shore. He collected big pieces of wood and threw them into the sea.

He had tied the pieces of wood to the ship so they would not float away. He pulled them closer and climbed down on to them.

He lashed four lengths of wood together, then tied more pieces across them. This made his raft strong enough to walk on.

6

Crusoe loaded the raft with the most useful things he could find – chests full of food, barrels of rum, guns and barrels of gunpowder.

Then, using a pole as a steering pole, he guided the raft towards the shore. He landed it on the beach and unloaded his cargo.

After eating some of the food, Crusoe climbed a hill to see where he was. At the top he looked round and saw he was on an island.

The next day he returned to the ship and collected more tools and clothes. To his delight, he also found the ship's dog and two cats.

Crusoe went back to the ship every day and soon had many useful things. He piled them up round a tent he had made from poles and sails.

One night there was another fierce storm. When Crusoe looked out of his tent the next morning, he saw that the ship had been washed away.

Crusoe looked for somewhere to live. He wanted to be near a stream and to have a view of the sea in case a ship ever passed by.

He soon found a good place. It was a flat space up on a hill facing the sea. At the back was a steep cliff with a cave at the bottom of it.

First Crusoe built a fence. He cut up wood to make posts and drove them into the ground in a semi-circle in front of the cave.

Before finishing the fence, he carried his stores up to the cave. When the fence was complete he made a ladder so he could climb over it.

Inside the fence Crusoe set up a large tent of wood and sails he had saved from the ship. First he made a small tent, then he built a bigger

one over it, to protect it from the rain. This was to be his home. But as he also wanted a dry store room, he decided to enlarge the cave.

8

First he needed a spade. He found a tree with very hard wood and cut off a branch. Then he carefully carved it into the shape of a spade.

To make the cave bigger, he dug out earth and sand. He piled the earth against the inside of the fence to make it stronger.

During the new few weeks Crusoe made his cave more comfortable. He made a table and a chair from planks he had saved from the ship.

He had never done any carpentry before but he found that if he worked slowly he could manage to make anything he wanted.

Crusoe soon settled down to life on the island. Every morning he went out hunting with his dog, to shoot birds or wild goats for food.

Sometimes he climbed the cliffs to look for seabirds' nests in cracks in the rocks. The birds flew round as he collected the eggs.

At mid-day he went home and cooked his food over a fire. He skinned all the animals he caught or shot and dried the skins to use later.

It was too hot to work in the afternoons, so Crusoe slept in a hammock he had made, tied between two poles in his tent.

Later, when it was cooler, he started work again on more things for the cave. Everything took him a long time but he did not mind.

In the evenings Crusoe wrote his diary. He lit the cave with candles he had made, which were wicks floating in dishes of goat's fat.

Crusoe did not want to lose count of the days while he was on the island, so he made a sort of calendar with a pole he set up on the beach.

Every day he cut a notch in the pole. For Sundays and the first day of a month he cut longer notches, so that he always knew the date.

One day Crusoe shook out an old corn sack he found among his things. There was very little corn left in it and he wanted to use the sack.

Months later he found ripe corn growing. Crusoe picked it and kept the grain to plant later, so he could grow enough corn for bread.

One day, when Crusoe was in his cave, the ground shook and rocks crashed down the cliff. Terrified, Crusoe ran outside. It was an earthquake. When it was over, a huge storm blew up. Crusoe crept back to his cave. He felt very lucky to be still alive.

11

When Crusoe had been on the island for ten months he set off to explore it. He took his gun in case he met any savages or wild animals.

In the middle of the island, he came to a green valley where orange trees grew. "I will build a home here one day," he thought.

Vines heavy with grapes grew in the valley. Crusoe picked as many grapes as he could carry. Later he dried them in the sun to make raisins.

There were many parrots in that part of the island. Crusoe knocked a young one down from a tree and took it home with him.

He made the parrot a perch and spent hours teaching it to talk. After a while it could say "Robinson" and its own name, "Poll".

One day Crusoe shot a baby goat by mistake. He took it home to look after it and it became tame. Crusoe now had several pets.

Just before the rainy season Crusoe planted his corn. Soon he had a fine cornfield. He built a fence round it to keep out the wild goats.

Then birds began to peck at the corn. Crusoe shot a few and hung them on posts round the field to scare away away other birds.

Crusoe needed something to keep his corn in, so he made pots from clay and dried them in the sun. The first ones were not very round.

One day a pot fell in the fire. Then Crusoe found that if he baked his pots they would hold water and he could use them for cooking.

When Crusoe had cut his corn he was ready to make bread. He ground the corn into flour, then mixed it with water to make a dough.

He put loaves of dough on to tiles and covered them with bowls. He laid them in hot ashes to cook, and soon he had baked his first loaves.

One day, as Crusoe was exploring the island, he came to some high cliffs. He looked out to sea and, to his surprise, saw land on the horizon. He did not know if it was the mainland or another island. Suddenly he felt lonely and wanted to escape from his island.

He went to look at a boat which had been washed ashore in a storm. He tried to push it down to the sea but it was too heavy.

He decided to make himself a boat like an Indian canoe. He went into the woods and chose a straight tree growing on the edge of the beach.

He cut it down and trimmed off the branches. This took him a long time. Then he hollowed out the trunk, using tools from the ship.

After many weeks the canoe was finished. It was huge. Crusoe was proud of it. "It is big enough to carry all my stores," he thought.

But Crusoe had built his boat a long way from the sea and he could not move it. He began to dig a canal so he could float it down to the sea, but he soon realised it would take him years. All his work was wasted. Sadly he stopped digging and gave up any idea of escape.

Crusoe had now been on the island for four years and his clothes were in rags. He had no cloth for new ones but he had plenty of goatskins.

He had stretched all the goatskins over sticks and hung them up to dry. He sewed them together to make trousers, a jerkin and a hat.

The new clothes looked very odd, but Crusoe was pleased with them. They protected him from the fierce sun and the tropical rain.

Crusoe also made an umbrella. He used sticks for the frame and goatskins for the cover. On hot days he used it as a sunshade.

Crusoe still wanted a boat and after a while he made another one. It was smaller than the first one and this time he built it by the sea.

Crusoe knew he could not sail to the mainland. The boat was too small for that. He just wanted to sail all round the island.

When he had finished the boat, Crusoe stocked it with food for the voyage – loaves of bread, meat, raisins and water.

He fixed his umbrella up at the back of the boat to shade him from the hot sun and he put his gun in a safe place. Then he set sail.

The sun was shining and the there was a good breeze to fill the sail. Crusoe steered along the coast, carefully avoiding rocks.

He stopped in a small bay and went ashore. He climbed a hill to look around and noticed there were dangerous currents out at sea.

Crusoe set off again, staying close to the shore. But he had not gone far when the boat was suddenly caught in a strong current.

Crusoe lowered the sail and struggled to row against the current, but it was no use. He was being swept far out to sea.

Suddenly the wind changed. Crusoe put up his sail and found that he was being blown out of the current and back towards the island.

When he reached the coast, he staggered ashore and fell on his knees to thank God he was safe. Then he walked back across the island.

As soon as he was home, he climbed into his hammock and fell asleep. Suddenly he was woken up by a voice calling his name. Frightened,

he grabbed his gun and sat up. Then he laughed. Perched in front of him was his parrot. "Poor Robin Crusoe," it squawked cheerfully.

Pole I set up on the beach to mark the other side of the island

Beach where there are many turtles

Cove where I keep my boat

My country home

High cliffs from which I can see land

Paddock where I keep my goats

Look-out point

My cornfield

Stream

My fortress

Calendar pole

Sandbank on which the ship was wrecked

The cliff I first climbed

My raft

The rocks I was swept on to

This is the map of the island that Crusoe drew after he had sailed round it.

He marked on it all the places he knew and added more as he went exploring.

18

Dangerous currents
out at sea

Rocky
point

first
at I
ade

N
W — E
S

After he had been on the
island for a few years,
Crusoe built a summer home
in the valley where the
orange trees grew.

He made a tent and planted
young trees round it. They
grew fast and gave plenty of
shade. It was a cool place
to spend hot summer days.

Crusoe kept his goats in a
paddock next to his summer
home. He caught his first
goats in a pit trap and
soon tamed them.

They had kids and after a
year Crusoe had a whole
flock of goats. He milked
them and made butter and
cheese from their milk.

Crusoe had been on the island for twelve years and was quite content. He had all he wanted and felt like the king of the island.

Then one day he saw a foot print on the beach. He stopped, listened and stared all round him but he could not hear or see anyone.

Terrified, he ran home. He dared not look back. He was sure he was being followed and that savages were lurking behind every bush.

He hid in his fortress for days, too scared to come out. Then he wondered if he was being silly. "Perhaps it is my foot print," he thought.

He went back to the beach and measured his foot against the print. The print was larger. A stranger must have been on the island.

Crusoe rushed home. He made his fence stronger and fixed guns in it. He planted trees round his fortress so they would grow and hide it.

20

Another year passed and Crusoe did not see anyone. Then one morning, as he walked along a beach, he stopped in horror. On the ground were the remains of a fire and round it were human bones. Crusoe felt sick. Cannibals, man-eating savages, had been there.

Crusoe did not feel safe any more. He was sure the cannibals would return. He found a hiding place and looked out to sea every day.

One day, when he was cutting wood, he found a cave. "No one would find my guns and gunpowder here," he thought.

He walked into the cave, then ran out in fright. Two eyes were shining at him out of the darkness. Perhaps it was a cannibal.

Crusoe plucked up his courage. He lit a torch and went back into the cave. Then he laughed. "It's only a poor old goat," he said.

21

Months went by and Crusoe did not see any savages. Then early one morning he saw the light of a fire on the beach. He ran home.

He loaded his guns in case the cannibals found his corn field and came looking for him. But he wanted to know what was going on.

He crept back to the beach to watch. Nine savages were dancing round a fire and feasting. When they had finished, they got into

their canoes and paddled away towards the mainland. Crusoe was glad to see them go. From then on he looked out for them every day.

One night after this there was a bad storm. Crusoe was in his cave, reading a book he had found on the ship. Suddenly he heard a gunshot.

He knew he could not help
the people on the ship, but
hoped they might be able to
rescue him. He lit a fire
on the cliffs as a beacon.

But when day broke, he saw
the ship was wrecked. His
heart sank. He could not
escape now. He hoped there
would be some survivors.

He ran out to the look-out
point on the cliff. A flash
of lightning lit the sky
and Crusoe saw a ship
tossing on the stormy seas.

He sailed out to the wreck
but, to his dismay, found
that there was no one alive
on board. He would have to
remain alone on the island.

Most of the ship's cargo had
been spoiled by sea water.
Crusoe found a chest full of
gold. "What use is gold to
me?" he asked himself sadly.

23

Suddenly the second captive broke away from the group and ran away towards the woods. Two of the cannibals chased after him.

Two years went by peacefully, then Crusoe saw five canoes on the beach near his home. He crept closer to look. About thirty savages were roasting meat over a fire and two captives were waiting to be killed. As Crusoe watched, the savages hit one captive on the head.

Crusoe ran home and fetched his guns. He wanted to save the captive. "He could keep me company," he thought and hurried back to the beach.

As soon as the three savages were out of sight of the cannibals on the beach, Crusoe ran out towards them. They stopped, surprised by this man in goatskins. Crusoe ran up to one of the pursuers and hit him so hard on the head with his gun that he fell down dead.

The second savage pulled back his bow to shoot, but Crusoe was too quick for him. He fired his gun and killed him instantly.

The captive stopped running when he saw his enemies were dead and stared at Crusoe. Crusoe smiled and beckoned, to show he was friendly.

The captive slowly came forwards, then knelt and kissed the ground at Crusoe's feet. This meant he wanted to be Crusoe's servant.

After burying the savages in the sand, Crusoe took the man home with him. He gave him food, then the tired savage fell asleep.

Next day Crusoe began to teach the savage English. He taught him his name was Friday, as that was the day on which he had been saved.

Crusoe and Friday went to the beach. The cannibals had gone. Friday pointed to the graves. He wanted to dig up the savages and eat them.

Crusoe was very angry. He tried to show that the thought of eating people made him feel sick. Friday understood and looked sad.

Back at the fortress, Crusoe gave Friday some clothes. Friday was proud of them, but felt uncomfortable. He had not worn clothes before.

Crusoe decided to teach Friday to eat animal meat. He took him hunting with him and shot a goat. The noise of the gun scared Friday.

He looked at his stomach to see if he had been hurt. He did not understand how the gun had killed the goat. He begged Crusoe not to kill him.

As time passed, Crusoe taught Friday to fire a gun, to help in the cornfield and to make bread. Friday was quick to learn.

He learned English and he and Crusoe told each other about their homes. Crusoe was glad to have someone to talk to at long last.

One clear day Friday saw the mainland. He was excited. "Look," he called to Crusoe, "There is my home. Let us make a boat and go there."

"I can't go," said Crusoe. "Your cannibal friends will eat me." "No," said Friday, "They will like you because you saved my life."

So Crusoe and Friday made a boat and Crusoe taught Friday how to sail it. They collected food for their voyage to the mainland.

Then one day Friday saw three canoes approaching the shore. The cannibals were back. Terrified, Friday ran to tell Crusoe.

27

"We must fight them," said Crusoe. He and Friday loaded the guns and shared out the weapons. Then they crept down to a wood by the beach.

Friday climbed a tree to see what was happening. Many savages were feasting round a fire. They had one captive. It was a white man.

Crusoe and Friday hid in the bushes near the beach. "Fire!" shouted Crusoe and they shot at the savages, killing some and wounding others.

The ones who were not hurt were terrified. They sprang to their feet but did not know where to run. Crusoe and Friday fired again.

Then they rushed out of the bushes. The savages ran towards the canoes, hoping to escape, but Friday chased them, firing his gun.

Crusoe ran to the captive and untied him. The captive was a Spaniard. Crusoe gave him a gun and told him to try and defend himself.

Soon they had killed all the savages except for three, who escaped in a canoe. "Quick," Crusoe shouted to Friday, "We must stop them."

He ran to a canoe and, to his surprise, found an old man lying in it, tied and gagged. As Crusoe untied him, Friday ran up to him.

When Friday saw the old man he shouted for joy, then rushed over to him and hugged him. "This is my father," he told Crusoe.

Friday's father and the Spanish captive were weak. Crusoe and Friday carried them back to the fortress so they could eat and rest.

The next day the Spaniard told Crusoe that there were more Spanish sailors on the mainland. "I must go back to them," he told Crusoe.

Crusoe gave him food and weapons and soon the Spaniard set sail for the mainland, taking Friday's father with him.

A week later, to his surprise, Crusoe saw an English ship moored off the coast. He wondered why it had come to the island.

Looking through his telescope, he saw a boat full of sailors coming in to land. Three of the sailors were prisoners.

The sailors left the boat on the beach and went off to explore the island, leaving the three prisoners tied up under a tree.

Crusoe and Friday walked down to the beach and went up to the prisoners. "Who are you?" Crusoe asked them gently. "Can we help you?"

The prisoners stared at Crusoe. "I was the captain of that ship," one said. "My sailors mutinied and are leaving us on this island."

"I will help you," said Crusoe, "if you take us to England after we recapture your ship." The captain agreed and Crusoe untied him.

As the sailors returned to the beach, they were seized. Crusoe told them that he would spare their lives if they swore to help him.

Soon more sailors came ashore. Seeing the boat but no one on the beach, they called out. Crusoe told Friday to lure them away.

Friday hid in the trees and answered the sailors' calls. Thinking he was one of their friends, they went looking for him and got lost.

As they looked for the way back to the beach, the captain's men ambushed them, tied them up and led them to Crusoe's fortress.

When it was dark, the captain rowed out to the ship with twelve trusted men. They quietly climbed aboard, then opened fire.

Taken by surprise, the rebels surrendered. The captain then fired a signal to let Crusoe know that the ship had been recaptured.

Next morning the captain rowed back to Crusoe. "The ship is yours," he said. Crusoe was delighted. At last he could leave the island.

The captain had presents for Crusoe, who put on his first proper clothes for many years. Then he, Friday and the captain had a great feast.

First published in 1981 by Usborne Publishing Ltd, 20 Garrick Street, London WC2 9BJ, England.

Published in Canada by Hayes Publishing Ltd, Burlington, Ontario.

Published in Australia by Rigby Publishing Ltd, Adelaide, Sydney, Melbourne, Brisbane.

Published in USA in 1981 by Hayes Books, 4235 South Memorial Drive, Tulsa, Oklahoma, USA.

Printed in Belgium by Casterman S.A.

They set sail for home and, after a long journey, finally reached England. Crusoe had been away thirtyfive years. The gold he had saved from the wreck made him a very rich man. Friday stayed with him for the rest of his days and they never forgot their life on the desert island.